ABOUT THE BANK STREET READY-TO-READ SERIES

More than seventy-five years of educational research, innovative teaching, and quality publishing have earned The Bank Street College of Education its reputation as America's most trusted name in early childhood education.

Because no two children are exactly alike in their development, the Bank Street Ready-to-Read series is written on three levels to accommodate the individual stages of reading readiness of children ages three through eight.

● *Level 1:*   **GETTING READY TO READ (Pre-K–Grade 1)**
Level 1 books are perfect for reading aloud with children who are getting ready to read or just starting to read words or phrases. These books feature large type, repetition, and simple sentences.

● *Level 2:*   **READING TOGETHER (Grades 1–3)**
These books have slightly smaller type and longer sentences. They are ideal for children beginning to read by themselves who may need help.

○ *Level 3:*   **I CAN READ IT MYSELF (Grades 2–3)**
These stories are just right for children who can read independently. They offer more complex and challenging stories and sentences.

All three levels of The Bank Street Ready-to-Read books make it easy to select the books most appropriate for your child's development and enable him or her to grow with the series step by step. The levels purposely overlap to reinforce skills and further encourage reading.

We feel that making reading fun is the single most important thing anyone can do to help children become good readers. We hope you will become part of Bank Street's long tradition of learning through sharing.

The Bank Street College of Education

For sweet Pete, my brother
—E.S.
For my husband, Warren,
with love
—B.W.

SLEEP TIGHT, PETE
A Bantam Book/March 1995

Published by Bantam Doubleday Dell Books
for Young Readers, a division of Bantam
Doubleday Dell Publishing Group, Inc.
1540 Broadway, New York, New York 10036.

Special thanks to Susan Schwarzchild,
Matt Hickey, Hope Innelli, and Kathy Huck.

The trademarks "Bantam Books" and the
portrayal of a rooster are registered
in the U.S. Patent and Trademark Office
and in other countries. Marca Registrada.

Library of Congress Cataloging-in-Publication Data
Schecter, Ellen.
Sleep tight, Pete / by Ellen Schecter ;
illustrated by Bari Weissman.
p. cm. — (Bank Street ready-to-read)
"A Byron Preiss book."
Summary: *Pete's mother tells him three bedtime stories*
in which he is the hero.
ISBN 0-553-09047-X (hardcover). — ISBN 0-553-37570-9 (pbk.)
[1. Bedtime—Fiction. 2. Storytelling—Fiction.]
I. Weissman, Bari, ill. II. Title. III. Series.
PZ7.S3423Sl 1995
[E]—dc20
94-9790 CIP AC

Published simultaneously in the United States and Canada

PRINTED IN THE UNITED STATES OF AMERICA

0 9 8 7 6 5 4 3 2 1

Bank Street Ready-to-Read™

Sleep Tight, Pete

by Ellen Schecter
Illustrated by Bari Weissman

A Byron Preiss Book

BANTAM BOOKS
NEW YORK • TORONTO • LONDON • SYDNEY • AUCKLAND

"Tell me some bedtime stories,"
said Pete.
He snuggled under his covers,
sticking both feet out
to catch the breeze.
"Tell me some stories about
me and you—just us two."
"Okay," said his mother.
"Here's one."

PETE AND THE BIG STICK

One day Pete skipped
into the kitchen while
his mom baked cookies.
"Can I go out and play?"
Pete asked.
"Sure," answered his mother.

"Can I throw sticks and stones
in the brook?" asked Pete.
"Sure," said his mom. "Have fun!"
Pete ran outside.
He found three twigs, two shiny
stones, and one big stick.

Pretty soon Pete came
back inside.
His shoes and shirt were soaked.
His pants were all muddy.
Even his hair was dripping wet.

"For Pete's sake!" said his mom.
She wiped her hands,
then wiped his tears.

She took him on her lap
and gave him a big hug.
Then she gave him
a big fat cookie,
still warm from the oven.

"What happened, sweet Pete?"
she asked.
"Well, I went out to the brook,"
said Pete.
"And I skipped some stones.
Then I threw three twigs."

"That sounds like fun,"
said his mom.
"But then I found a stick.
It was almost as big as me!
And I threw it in the brook,"
Pete said.

"So what happened next?"
asked his mom.
"I FORGOT TO LET GO!" said Pete.

"Oh, for Pete's sake!" said Mom.
She gave him a big fat hug—
wet clothes and all.

"Now tell me another story!"
Pete said.
Pete's mom smiled and began.

US ON THE BUS
One day Pete and his mother
rode home on a crowded bus.
All Pete could see were elbows,
and shopping bags, and knees.

13

It was a very long ride,
and Pete got very bored.
"Stop wiggling, sweet Pete,"
said his mom.
But it was hard to sit still.
So Pete turned into a cat.

14

"Meow," Pete said softly.
Nobody noticed.
"Meow! Meow!"
Pete said a bit louder.
Nobody said anything.

"MEOW-MEOW-MEOWWWW!"
yowled Pete.
He wanted someone to answer.
But some people looked angry.
One woman just yawned
and looked away.

16

MEOWWW!!

17

But Pete didn't stop.
"Meow," he said to his mother.
He stuck out his claws.
He wiggled his whiskers.
He meowed again.

18

"Please, Pete,"
his mother said softly.
"No meowing on the bus."
Then a lady tapped Pete's arm.

"Excuse me," she said.
"Did you meow?"
"Meow," answered Pete,
meaning "Yes."
"There's no meowing
on this bus," said the lady.

20

"But I'm a cat," Pete answered.
"Cats can't ride buses,"
the lady said.
"If you're a cat,
you'll have to get off."

Pete sat still and looked
out the window.
He saw people who looked
like their dogs
and dogs that looked
like their people.
Pete wiggled his whiskers.
He pulled in his claws.

Then the bus stopped
and got very quiet.
"Arf! Arf!" Pete barked,
wagging his tail to be friendly.
"For Pete's sake!"
laughed his mother.
"Thank goodness
the next stop is ours."

23

"Arf! Arf!" barked Pete.
"One more story? Please?"
"Okay, just one more!
Then it's sleep time," said Mom.

24

THE CASE OF THE MISSING MOM

One day, Pete trailed his mom
from room to room.
"Can we play hide-and-seek?"
he asked.
"After I mop the floor,
make the bed,
start the stew,
and slice the bread.
Then I'll play," she promised.

Pete watched his mom's busy
feet hurry back and forth
and up and down.
He watched her
mop and scrub and slice
and start the stew.
She was busy forever and ever.

Finally she called out,
"I'm ready!
I'll hide and you seek."
Pete counted to twenty
very, very slowly.

"Ready or not, here I come!"
yelled Pete.
But where was his mom?
Pete searched high and low.

He searched in the closet,
in the hall,
behind the curtains
near the wall.
Finally he spied the tip
of a shoe he knew.

The shoe led to a foot,
the foot led to a leg,
and the leg led to his
hard-working missing mom—
sound asleep with her arms
for a pillow.

"And then you kissed me up, like the Prince and Sleeping Beauty," said Mom. "Do you remember, Pete? Pete?"

Pete's mom hugged the lump
under the covers.
She kissed two sticking-out toes.
Then she smiled.
"For Pete's sake!"
she said softly.
Then she whispered,
"Sleep tight, Pete."
For Pete was sound asleep.